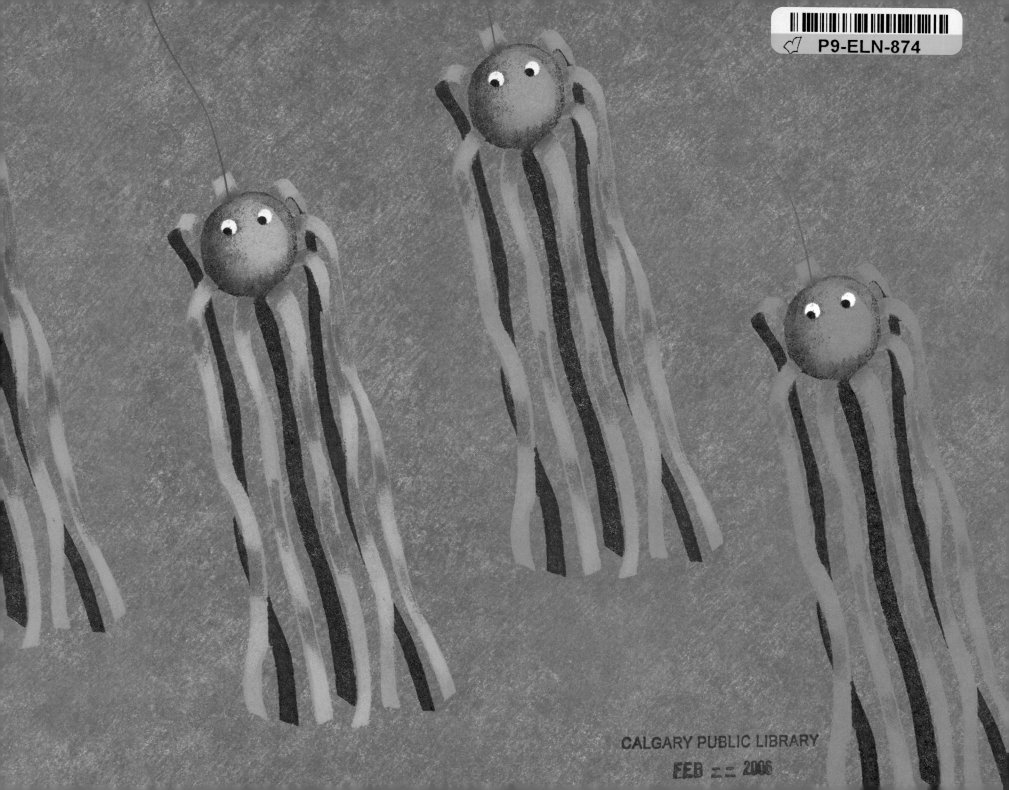

Come with Me on HALLOWEEN

Linda Hoffman Kimball   Illustrated by Mike Reed

Albert Whitman & Company, Morton Grove, Illinois

Library of Congress Cataloging-in-Publication Data

Kimball, Linda Hoffman.
Come with me on Halloween / by Linda Hoffman Kimball ; illustrated by Mike Reed.
p. cm.
Summary: As a father and his young son visit a scary Halloween haunted house and
then go trick-or-treating, it's unclear just who is helping whom be brave.
ISBN 0-8075-3132-4 (hardcover)
[1. Halloween—Fiction. 2. Haunted houses—Fiction. 3. Fathers and sons—Fiction.]
I. Reed, Mike, 1951- ill. II. Title.
PZ8.3.K55933Com 2005 [E]—dc22 2005004091

Text copyright © 2005 by Linda Hoffman Kimball.
Illustrations copyright © 2005 by Mike Reed.
Published in 2005 by Albert Whitman & Company,
6340 Oakton Street, Morton Grove, Illinois 60053-2723.
Published simultaneously in Canada by Fitzhenry & Whiteside, Markham, Ontario.
Printed in China through Colorcraft, Ltd., Hong Kong.
10 9 8 7 6 5 4 3 2 1

The art is rendered in a combination of traditional and digital media.
The design is by Carol Gildar and Mike Reed.

For more information about Albert Whitman & Company,
please visit our web site at www.albertwhitman.com.

For Albert Hoffman, Jr.,
who held my hand.—L.H.K.

For Jane, Alex, and Joe—M.R.

When the pumpkin faces flicker,
monsters snicker,
witches bicker—
come with me. You'll be all right
on this Halloweening night.

When the wicked winds are howling,
black cats yowling,
goblins prowling—

Halloween Party
Tonight

ring the bell, then hold on tight.
Ghastly greeters scream delight.
They can't hurt you. You're with me
on this spooky Hallow...

We walk in and shutters shudder,
candles sputter,
spiders flutter!
Cobwebs drape the chandelier.
Never fear. You've got me near.

Next a mummy starts untangling,
dead skin dangling, shackles jangling.
Skeletons jump out and jiggle,
while they do their bony wiggle—
lean and mean on Halloween!

So what if the stairs are creaking,
ghosts are peeking...

bats are shrieking?
We make a team—
no need to scream.

Zombie couples dart in, dancing,
so entrancing,
rats around their ankles prancing.
First the tango,
then the cha-cha—
scram before their spell has gotcha!

When weird waiters stagger, staring,
red eyes glaring,
we are daring.
Sampling bits of "Brains in Batter,"
"Stomach Splatters," "Boiled Bladders"
served on fine bone-china platters.

In the darkness, beasts are bowling, heads are rolling.
In the distance, bells are tolling.

With their final gloomy bong,
creatures know to move along,
house to house and door to door,
ravens cawing, "Nevermore!"

What a night! And what a haul!
The bag can hardly hold it all!
Goodbye creatures, cute and creepy...

Now I think we're
getting sleepy.

That should do it for the night.
See? It wasn't such a fright!
I told you things would be all right.
Just stick with me. No need to fear.

I'll take you, Dad, again next year!

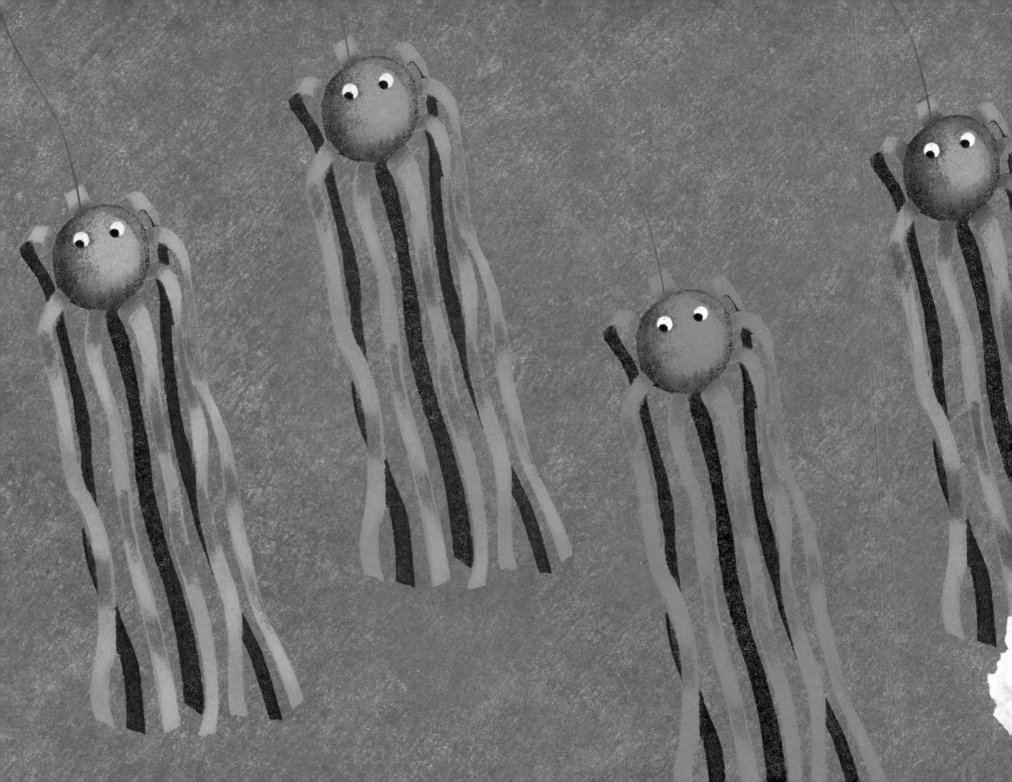